1975
MCMLXXV

Author:
Bill Webb

Editor:
Jeff Harkness

Layout:
Suzy Moseby

Front Cover Art:
Michael Syrigos

Cover Design
Jim Wampler

Cartography:
Robert Altbauer

Project Manager:
Zach Glazar

Frog God Games is:

Bill Webb, Matt Finch, Zach Glazar, Charles A. Wright, Edwin Nagy, Mike Badolato, and John Barnhouse

**ADVENTURES
WORTH
WINNING**

FROG GOD GAMES
ISBN: 978-1-62283-896-7
SW PoD

TABLE OF CONTENTS

1975

By Bill Webb

A Swords & Wizardry adventure designed for four to six characters of 1st to 3rd level

About Old School Gaming

This module is intended to show how old school roleplaying provides enhanced descriptions and provides not only storyline and encounters, but creates a feeling of "being there". I have borrowed from work I did supporting Matt Finch at North Texas RPG Con in 2011, as well as sessions I ran at PaizoCon in 2011 and 2012.

Rules in 1975 were few, people did not really understand roleplaying games as they do today, and we had to make them smell, hear and feel the stench of the dead body, the weird drumming sounds in the deep, and the cold, clammy touch of a ghoul's claw.

When the game was new, none of the players had read 100+ RPG books. They did not know if a dwarf was a 6-inch tall faerie or one of Tolkien's hardened miners with an axe and a love of gold. We had to tell them. As the game has evolved, we deal with a much more educated and cunning set of players. In order to stay a step ahead, the game master must create and describe many situations both hazardous and benign with equal enthusiasm. Players can be kept on their toes and edges of their seats by harmless blue flowers as well as deadly poisonous yellow flowers if they don't know which is which. The art of storytelling in our favorite game is not dead—heavens no—but to really get back to the roots of the game, it helps to provide mystery and fear.

Some players have joked with me over the years that they never know when to let up—and instead assume combat mode as soon as "flavor text" gets heavy. Having personally never been a fan of the "spot check" or a blind roll to "disarm the trap" without having it fully described, I use flavor text to allow players to creatively solve problems by asking questions and better understanding "what it is" that their characters see and do. Secret doors are not automatically opened…they must be examined, loose bricks and levers must be searched for, and so on. An orc is not just an orc. It could be a hairy humanoid, with jutting tusks and whitish green skin, barking in an obscene, unintelligible language while it charges at you with its rusted poleaxe! The troll does not simply "regenerate", but its wounds close over the arrows in its chest almost faster than the blood drips from them.

This is the stuff of 1975.

I have tried I this module to provide a Referee with enough information to improvise and make the most of description as a technique in his or her game. Resources exist (Tabletop Adventures, and our very own *Tome of Adventure Design* come to mind) to add to this as deemed needed. Its not the only way, nor the best way to play. It's just how I play, and I play *Swords and Wizardry*.

This adventure is designed for 4-6 characters of levels 1-4. The setting may seem fairly easy for characters above 1st level, however, I would enjoin upon the Referee to play his or her monsters to kill. Treat them as if they were your own player characters. A goblin with a bow would never get near Joe Platemail III with his huge sword and slow movement rate. A crocodile would grab a lightly armed opponent and drag them into the water—it would never stand and fight a group of 5 men toe to toe. Ghouls would paralyze one opponent and then move to the next, zombies would..well, ok, they would act like zombies and just stand there and attack.

Two things make fairly-played monsters in my games. One is that I play them as smart as they are, and the second is that I roll all dice openly on the table for all to see, and mandate that all do the same. Oddly, people think I am discouraging player cheating. In reality, I find (even in my own case at times) it's the DM who more frequently dances the dice to keep characters alive. Give these things a shot and see what the results are. I have found that the players are more in love with the challenge of the game and less in love with their characters. Likewise, a player who has reached higher levels (as high as 4!) has truly made an achievement.

On the player's side, it is of critical importance, at least to me, that they learn how to run as well as fight. As Gandalf said, "there is always something bigger in this world than yourself". Truly skilled old school players employed many means of evasion as well as tricky means of fighting the bad guys. Old rules even included methods for increasing odds (gold pieces thrown behind for intelligent monsters, food for the less intelligent monsters), and just because it was "there" did not mean you had to kill it—at least yet. Players would base entire game sessions and plans on taking out a single BEBG (big evil bad guy) that they had previously escaped from.

That is why speed, evasion and care are required. As experience points (XP) for slaying monsters are few, and for gathering loot are big, it made far more sense to avoid wasted resources by killing everything that crossed one's path, and instead staying goal focused and keeping one's eye on the ball. The big monsters (intelligent ones) have big treasure (and big XP). The bugs (and purple worms) have none.

A Note about Equipment

One of the things that was noticeably different in the old days was the clever use of all kinds of mundane gear in the dungeon and wilderness setting. There were no magic or semi magic (thunderstones etc.) items available for players to rely on as a "given". A single magic potion is a truly big deal. Iron spikes to temporarily bind doors, crowbars to crack open chests and lift gates, burning oil to block corridors, and 10-foot poles to prod ahead in corridors all were a major part of the game. *What* you took with you into the dark deeps of the dungeon often meant the difference between death and survival. After all, when trying to block the crypt door from the incoming group of orcs, a certain famous fantasy figure used an old poleaxe to wedge the door so that his friends could loose several rounds of arrows into the horde before melee was joined. Effective.

Often players would come up with truly ingenious uses for seemingly simple materials to delay, confound or catch monsters. Likewise, monsters like kobolds would use scorpions on long poles, a series of traps and even oil to fight back against the big, bad adventurers. Its up to the Referee to determine what works and what does not work. I always apply a reasonableness standard to each idea. A good Referee can have the monsters educate the players by using this type of trick (perhaps dropping flaming oil on both sides of a corridor and shooting arrows at the players and then running away?). Pretty soon, the players will be doing the same to your precious pet monsters.

A Note about Character Stats

Unlike many versions of the game, character stats in *Swords and Wizardry* do not have a tremendous effect on game play. Most stats grant a maximum of +1 to any die roll. The one exception is the high strength fighter attacking or a high dexterity fighter in parry mode (grants a maximum -4 bonus to armor class, although in this case, he cannot also attack).

What stat bonuses did to the game (not a good or bad thing, just a thing), was create a power creep first for characters (+6 damage on a d6 weapon is +200% average damage, for example), and later for monsters as the Referee had to create bigger and badder foes just to create a level playing field.

This in turn lead to extremely powerful characters even at low levels, and led to what is today the 4 page, 2 hour character creation phase of many games. Character creation in *Swords and Wizardry* takes about 5 minutes maximum. The characters are far more defined in the player's mind than what is on the piece of paper they are using as a character record sheet.

A Note about Experience Points and Advancement

Experience in *Swords and Wizardry* works a little different than in more modern iterations of the game. Monsters are worth very little experience, and treasure rules. Typically, 1 gold piece translates to 1 experience point (xp). What this means to the Referee is that one must be fairly stingy with the gold pieces in one's campaign, else the characters will become high level in short order. This does not mean you cannot give out treasure, it just means that you need to make the players work for it.

In the First Edition Dungeon Master's Guide, Gary Gygax wrote a wonderful treatise on a 2000 gp treasure. It contained no gold pieces, and the highest value item was 300 gp (a piece of jewelry). To garner those 2000 xp, the players would have to carefully figure out how to extract value out of the random equipment, foodstuffs, spices and fancy items, find buyers, and convert them to gold. This required interaction with NPCs—be it shops, other adventurers or innkeepers ("I'll give you this tanned beaver pelt instead of the 5 gp for the week at the inn").

A suit of platemail is a wonderful treasure—it's worth lots of xp *as long as the players can find a buyer*! A jeweled cup might be worth 10 gp (and 10 xp) or it might be worth 100 gp (and 100 xp!). It all depends on what the players can sell it for (or realize value from them in barter).

I typically use creative treasures. Rarely will my players find 200 gp and a 400 gp gem. They are much more likely to find 3 barrels of fine ale (worth 15 gp each), a slightly rusty suit of chainmail with an intricately engraved coat of arms (worth 40 gp or 200 gp if sold back to the noble family that owns the coat of arms), 2 longswords, a bardiche, a suit of leather barding, 12 oil flasks, a backpack full of fine silk (60 gp worth), 422 sp, 110 cp, and a set of platinum earrings set with rubies in the shape of tiny birds (worth 75 gp).

Its about the same total value, but the players may only get 43 xp (the coins) or much more if they cleverly sell the gear and trinkets. Likewise, during treasure distribution, a player may really want that magic potion—but if he takes the potion (0 xp) he may have to let the other players take the monetary treasure and thus gain xp. It's a tough decision.

Money = xp. It is irrelevant how the individual player (experience is by a person, not the group) gets it. The only exception is that no xp should be awarded from gold gained from other player characters, not even for selling their gear if killed.

Monster experience is typically very low. While *Swords and Wizardry* dictates xp for killing monsters, in my own campaign I typically award much less. My standard is 1 xp per hit point for normal monsters, and 2-3 times that if the monster possesses significant special abilities. For example, a bandit may have 5 hp, and carries 30 gp worth of gear (money, a bow, leather armor, and some minor treasure-like items). The bandit is worth 5-35 xp—5 if just killed and left in the field, but up to 35 if the players take his stuff and sell it for full value. Not bad for a 1 HD, 5 hp critter.

Alternatively, a giant centipede has no treasure, and 2 hp. I would award 4 xp for killing on (2 hp, doubled for poison). A medusa with 32 hp would be worth 96 xp (assuming she carried no treasure), since a stone gaze is a very powerful ability—hence 3x her value.

Unlike many versions of the game, player characters gain power in *Swords and Wizardry very* slowly. The game is designed so that a 10th level player character is very, very rare. In my original game back in the late 1970's and early 1980's, the characters reached 8-9th level after 2-3 years of weekly play. This is not to say that every Referee should provide for such slow advancement, but I have to tell you, the player skill gained by this slow crawl through levels was extreme. Frankly I have never played with more skilled, dare I say it, "opponents". These guys became expert in hit and run tactics, evasion of monsters, and "getting the maximum reward with the least risk. One time they drew a troll off on a wild goose chase while the thieves looted its lair. On another occasion, they drew unaligned monsters (a cockatrice and an ogre) towards each other so that the monsters would kill (or weaken) each other. Clever play.

They avoided fights, only attacked when they had a tactical advantage, and usually came away with the bulk of the rewards. They used their brains to advance rather than their brawn. The focus of their play was to 1) keep everyone alive, 2) get treasure and xp, and 3) rob monsters rather than fight when possible. Sure, they killed plenty of bad guys, but the focus was on winning, not killing.

Again, none of these are rules—it's just "a" way to play, albeit one I have found very rewarding.

A Note About Magic Items and Magic Item Creation

In old school games, magic item creation was virtually impossible. This made magic items rare to an extreme, and created situations where a single *+1 sword* was a huge treasure. High level (7-8th) characters might have 3-4 minor items. Certainly, no extremely powerful items graced their gear sheets. The unique items frequently were the whole object of a quest or series of adventures.

I have always treated magic items in the same way that later versions of the game have treated artifacts. They can be found mostly in the dark places of the earth, and the current owners typically use them when they fight. Certainly minor potions and scrolls do pop up now and again, as do the random minor item—but anything of great power (think vorpal sword, or wand) usually are rare and only found in dungeons. Characters would have to go to great lengths to get them, and get out alive again.

Magic item creation in some versions of the game has created a situation where even low level characters have access to potions, scroll, wands and even minor miscellaneous items on a regular basis. This in my mind has created two things—1) magic items found in treasure a "ho-hum, another +1 sword" and 2) power gaming has risen to an extreme. It's hard to challenge a group of 3rd level characters with a 3rd level monster if they are all decked out with magic weapons and potions. That causes the Referee to increase the levels (or magic items) that each monster has to catch up, then the players kill it, get more magic items, and the Referee has to again increase the monsters power quotient.

Honestly, I have seen this spiral out of control in many games in which I have played or run (I actually did run a 3E campaign to see how the game was played for a few months). In an age of CCG and MMO power players, it can get pretty out of control pretty fast when every character quaffs a potion and reads a scroll before every boss fight.

Swords and Wizardry plays a bit differently. Only very high-level characters (typically wizards and clerics) can make magic items. Magic item creation takes a long time, and costs the player a great deal of time in terms of research, gold and consultation with sages etc. This means that to forge that *+1 sword*, a wizard may not be able to adventure for several months (not gaining xp with his buddies that whole time). He may have to hire dwarven artisans to craft the sword from a special meteoric iron that costs its weight in gold. Finally, crafting the final incantations in to the sword could fail, ruining the whole process and losing time and money.

Minor items such as scrolls and potions are easier to make for sure—but still take time and money. I have applied a standard of 7th level for potions and scrolls, and of 12th level for other items as the minimum caster levels required to create items. Again, not a hard and fast rule (akin to AD&D rules—and taken from them!), but it has worked well for me. Look for an upcoming book from Frog God Games detailing some rules for this topic.

A final word on this—magic items should be very scarce in *Swords and Wizardry* games. The power level of both characters and monsters is quite low compared to most other versions of the game. Remember, an ancient red dragon only has 88 hp! It is not much of a challenge if both party wizards have crafted wands of lightning bolt at 5th level and can do 40 points of damage a round to the dragon.

A Note About Use of Non-Player Characters and Henchmen

One difference I have noted in the past few years is that few players heavily invest in the hiring and upkeep of henchmen, hirelings, and (with the exception of druids and rangers) pets. In the old days, most parties of characters would have a retinue of crossbowmen, spearmen, torchbearers, pack animals (see treasure above) and fighting pets (usually dogs). Henchmen differ in that they are actually class-based characters and can advance in level with the player characters.

Sure this costs them xp (I always divide monster xp by number of combatants total), and it caused them to expend those hard earned gold pieces, but it gave them both cannon fodder and increased capacity to go on extended dungeon and wilderness crawls.

Having 3 extra bowmen to shoot at the bandits with, or having those 3 pack mules to lug those kegs of ale became very important. Equally important was keeping morale of the retinue up (by overpayment, rewards and loyalty to one's henchmen). Lastly, this created a situation where the oft forgotten Charisma score of the characters was trivialized by many players. Simply put, a high charisma character who spread a lot of cash around to his retinue, shared the spoils of war with them, and healed or raised them when hurt or killed created a loyal following that would fight, protect and even die for their liege.

Likewise, poor treatment, a failure to heal or pay these hirelings, as well as a poor track record for keeping them alive created situations where no one would work for the characters; else charge exorbitant amounts for service, or even steal or betray them. NPC loyalty had to be kept in mind by the Referee so as not to allow an assumption of fanaticism create a situation where players could abuse the game with 20 archers in every encounter.

One other note on this, especially as it relates to pets. Scary stuff scares the retinue. A dog, even a highly trained attack dog, would run in terror from something undead or unnatural. A henchman would not stand and fight a medusa once it realized what it was. Players are responsible for dictating fear or lack thereof for themselves, but the Referee needs to consider what reaction the ex-farmhand torchbearer would have on facing a dragon.

A Note about Character Death and Resurrection

One fact about *Swords and Wizardry*, as well as old-school games in general exists. Player characters die. Frequently.

Since character creation is so rapid, it is not a problem to re-integrate a slain player in to a party. That being said, as a Referee (and I am always looking for ways to eat up that gold the players keep getting), I have never been opposed to allowing characters to be healed or raised from the dead by the local temple. Certainly the priests will charge a fair fee for this, and would refuse to cast a spell on a character of opposite alignment or a known criminal; but in general, the game lends itself to the need for NPC priests to bring a dead character back on occasion.

This is not to say that you as the Referee should make it easy or automatic—however this game Referee at least does make it available. I typically charge the players 1000 gp for a raise dead, and apply other fees for spells such as *cure disease, blindness*, etc. as needed. I also subtract these costs from the xp-driven treasure gained from the adventure. Keep in mind that not all towns have a priest who can raise the dead. It can be the whole point of an adventure just to get the dead PC to a locale where a priest can raise him. Then there is always the option of a *geas* or *quest* in lieu of fee. I love those spells. Level drain is a bit more permanent (and requires a 7th level spell to reverse—so fear those wights and wraiths!).

—BILL WEBB

The Adventure

Now that you, as the reader are sick of hearing this old grognard's lectures of how he runs the game, it's time to get on with the adventure. I have tried to illustrate several of the concepts I discussed above into examples of play and a scenario that will challenge and reward players for using their noggins.

The adventure begins with the characters finding a treasure map that leads them through a forested section of a river valley and down into the swamplands below. The map itself shows the general path to the "treasure" (in reality a small dungeon). The path taken to the dungeon may vary depending on the player's choices of travel—the Referee's map is coded with locations of the various encounters and other areas of interest that they could find. No path is the "right" path, although some may be easier than others.

The players map is found in the back of the book, and can be copied and given to them as a handout. The Judges map varies slightly in that it contains the map key detailing various encounter areas, and the players map just shows a dotted line. How the characters get the map is up to you as a Judge. Perhaps it was sold to the characters by a grizzled old man, or found as part of another treasure hoard. In any case, the introduction to "how" they start the adventure is not detailed here.

The adventure begins as the characters leave the (tavern, town etc.) and start down the road towards a valley. The valley itself is horseshoe-shaped, and the road the characters are on is near the top. The treasure map indicates that the "treasure" is in the bottom of the valley along a swampy river course, and is located on an island within the swamp itself. The trick is to find a safe way through the valley to reach the swamp, then to locate the island and the treasure (really s small dungeon). The encounter areas are located on the map, and can be used if the players travel near them.

Random Encounters

Random encounter checks should be made twice per day and twice per night. One way to handle this is to roll 1d12 per day and per night to randomize the hour (1 = 6 am, 12 = 5 pm at day, and 1 = 6 pm and 12 =5 am at night) to determine when the check is made. A random encounter typically occurs on a 1/20 chance. Forests add 1 to this roll (encounter chance 2/20) and swamps add 3 to the roll (encounter chance 4/20). Encounter tables are organized by terrain and are as follows:

Plains above the Valley (roll 1d12)

1. Circling Birds. The characters see a group of birds circling a mile distant. One by one, the birds drop to the ground. If approached, and before they can see what the birds are doing, they smell the cloying odor of rotting flesh. The birds sit pecking at the corpse of a large elk. [If the characters approach the carcass, add:] the birds squawk and shift around the body but do not give up their feast. One, sitting on the head of the dead creature, eyes them balefully.

2. Weird Snowfall. The characters wake in the morning to find that all the ground is white. Lying over everything is a layer of white stuff that looks like snow. But the moment they move, it shifts and rises in ways snow never does. As they brush it off, it hovers in the air, gradually settling. There are thousands of tiny seeds, each surrounded by a gossamer sphere of tiny white fluff that helps it float lightly in the air. They came, apparently, from the great tree (cottonwood) and covered the ground, plants, and people. They get into everything, though they do no damage. They are annoying to breathe but are only very dense right around the tree. Within a short time, although one or two can be seen still floating on the breeze; most have dispersed with the wind.

3. Falling Star (Only at night, else reroll). The night sky is bright and clear here in the grasslands. The stars themselves twinkle like diamonds in the void. Shooting stars race through the night, first white and then darkening to orange. It looks as if they will fall to earth here and perhaps bring luck and fortune with them, but they always just disappear before they come to earth. Sometimes shooting stars do come to earth and great good fortune is said to favor those who find one. Well, fortune is certainly smiling on the players as a rock the size of a large dog sits not far from the campsite. The rock is still glowing slightly and there is a trail of blackened, scorched grass to show where it initially landed and then slid along the ground perhaps as much as fifty paces. It is too hot to handle at the moment and a rock that size is very heavy, but it is well-known that the iron from meteors can be used to make superior steel and swords made from it may have a telling advantage. (Two long swords or four shorter blades could be made from the meteor, if it can be successfully brought to a suitably skilled blacksmith. Those weapons may at the GM's discretion have a +1 bonus in combat or else just be light, flexible and well-formed.). The meteor is found only once, although shooting stars can be a recurring encounter.

4-5. Bandits (2d4). Bandits are usually looking to ambush travelers, and there is a 1-3/6 chance that they surprise the group. If no surprise is indicated, or if the encounter occurs in the late afternoon or evening, the bandits may be in camp, in which case the party can surprise them on a 1-4/6. If they party has surprise, this can be played in several ways. One idea is to have the group spot a smoke trail (from the bandit's campfire). Bandits typically have leather armor, bows and hand weapons. The have 1d8 hp, and carry 2d6 gp of random loot each. The bandit camp contains foodstuffs and camp gear. There is a 10% chance that each bandit carries an oil flask (and torch) for use against heavily armored opponents.

Bandit: HD 1; AC 7[12]; Atk 1 weapon (1d6) or bow (1d6); Move 12; Save 17; CL/XP 1/15; Special: None; Gear: Leather armor, bow, hand weapon, 2d6 gp of random loot.

6. Wolves (2d6). Wolves seldom attack a party (unless wounded are present, or the characters number less than 1/3 the wolves number) during the day. At night, the wolves surprise 1-4/6, and attempt to gang attack 1-2 characters in hopes of a quick kill and drag off attempt. If the party has horses, the wolves attempt to kill one and then run off a short distance, having learned that dead animals are often left behind by human groups.

Wolf: HD 2+2; AC 7[12]; Atk 1 bite (1d4+1); Move 18; Save 16; CL/XP 2/30; Special: None.

7. Trade Caravan. These encounters typically involve 2d6 wagons and are accompanied by 1d8 armed men and 2 merchants/drivers per wagon (also armed). Guards are armed with crossbows and hand weapons and typically wear chainmail. Goods range in value from 10-100 gp per wagon and usually include items of value to local villages (cloth, metal goods and sundries, farm equipment, food and drink). There is a 10% chance that the caravan is carrying adventuring supplies (such as arms or armor). If so, the number of guards is doubled. Caravans are happy to sell (at 125% of book values) or buy (at 25% of book values) items from players. Each merchant carries from 20-200 gp in cash.

Caravan Guard/Merchant: HD 3; AC 5[14]; Atk 1 weapon (1d6) or heavy crossbow (1d6 + 1); Move 12; Save 15; CL/XP 3/60; Special: None; Gear: Chainmail, heavy crossbow, hand weapon.

8-9. Herd Animals. A herd of deer, wild cattle or otherwise innocuous beasts is spooked by the characters and runs by. Fast thinking players can shoot arrows and get a few free meals (assume each animal is AC 7[12] and has 2d6 hp).

10. Insect Swarm. One of the characters accidentally steps on a nest of hornets or otherwise nasty, biting insects. This is treated as if an insect plague spell had been cast, centered on a random player character.

11. Crazy Person. A slightly unstable old man or woman is lost/wandering about in the wilderness. The Referee can have fun with this one; perhaps the old lady is carrying a fishing pole and casting into the grass, or the old geezer is digging a large hole with a shovel, trying to unearth a "treasure" or "dungeon" and asks for help. Lawful groups would likely attempt to return the innocent to their home (usually <4 hours away). It would be a chaotic act to slay them.

Crazy Person: HD 1; AC 9[10]; Atk 1 weapon (1d6); Move 12; Save 17; CL/XP 1/15; Special: None; Gear: Odd implements.

12. Ankheg. This large preying mantis-like insect surprises foes on a 1-3/6, attacking from below. If it fails to surprise the characters, they notice mounds of disturbed dirt present on the ground and can avoid or ambush the beast instead. The huge insect has no treasure, however, it's hide can be used to make one suit of leather armor equivalent to chainmail (AC 5[14]) by a skilled armor worker.

Ankheg: HD 3; AC 2[17] underside 4[15]; Atk 1 bite (3d6); Move 12 (Burrow 6); Save 14; CL/XP 4/120; Special: Spits acid for 5d6 damage (1/day, save for half).

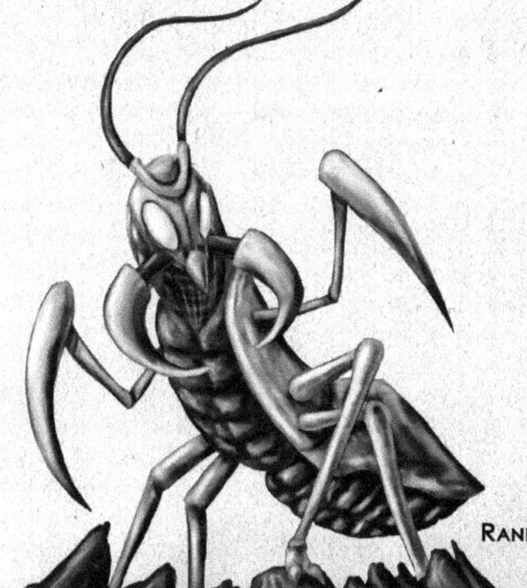

Forest in the Valley (roll 1d12)

1. Storm. A bolt of lightning lances down from the sky, squarely striking a small tree nearby. A shower of small wood chips fly about as the tree virtually explodes under the electrical onslaught. A few gray clouds have gathered overhead, but nothing to indicate a storm. A gigantic flash of lightning is followed immediately by a deafening clap of thunder and with a rush, the rain starts. The water pelts down mercilessly, instantly soaking everything. The rain drips under armor and through clothing. Gusts of wind whip through the grass, swirling it wildly. For a few moments, the rain comes down so hard vision is reduced to 10 feet. Overhead, the sky has grown completely black with thick clouds, and each flash of lightning illuminates the boiling mass of thunderheads above. Lightning and thunder are now virtually simultaneous, and each boom shakes the ground. The torrent continues for what feels like hours, and then quickly dies off with a few final stinging drops. The rain passes, though the clouds overhead promise to deliver more. Flashes of lightning still burst in the sky, but the thunder sounds farther away. The sky has a sickly greenish-yellow cast to it, turning the clouds an unearthly shade. After some time, a sudden change takes place. The clouds darken and the wind begins whipping ferociously. Sheets of rain fall from the sky drenching everything, followed closely by heavy hail. (Characters should be taking shelter in low areas or protected places at this point.) Lightning streaks across the sky; the black clouds are piled high above you. A roaring sound is heard and the ground begins to shake. A writhing, grey finger of cloud begin to descend from the sky towards the earth. As it touches down, the dust of the fields mushrooms up around its base. Like a snake preparing to strike, the storm writhes its way on a parallel course to your own, spreading destruction in its wake (a tornado). The characters are safe as long as they stay under cover.

2. Loud birds. The woods are filled with birdsong today. From the lilting twitters of tiny, brightly feathered finches to the throaty calls of surly crows, the birds all seem to be trying to outdo each other in volume and persistence. Above there are glimpses of the singers darting away from the group to continue their serenades from more secluded branches. The music is at times lovely, other times cacophonous. The one thing it never is, is silent.

3-4. Kobolds (2d4). These nasty little buggers are full of tricks and surprises. If not surprised, the kobolds will either flee (if no surprise) or ambush (if they have surprise) the party with missiles and traps. Each kobold carries 2 javelins, a club and one of the following:

- A poisonous snake on a 5 foot pole (snake is 2 hp, attacks separately, save at +2 or die)
- 1d2 oil flasks and a torch and tinder box
- Caltrops (50% chance if passing through a 5-foot area to take 1d2 damage and movement slowed to ¼ until damage is healed)
- A thin leather trip rope, 10 feet long
- Has a trap set nearby and tries to lead a character into it (see encounter 10 below).
- A flask of (1-3) Blood (4-5) vile feces or (6) green slime

Kobolds will hit and run, and will not engage the "big people" unless they clearly have an advantage. They carry no treasure.

Kobold: HD 1d4 hp; AC 6[13]; Atk 1 club (1d4) or 1 javelin (1d6); Move 6; Save 18; CL/XP A/5; Special: None; Gear: 2 javelins, 1 club.

5-6 Large Spiders (1d4). These nasty critters typically attack from above. If surprise is not indicated, the party sees webbing in the trees before the spiders attack. They have no treasure.

Large Spider: HD 1+1; AC 8[11]; Atk 1 bite (1 hp + poison); Move 9; Save 17; CL/XP 3/60; Special: Lethal poison (+2 saving throw).

7. Worgs (1d2). These evil wolves hunt the forest, slaying all they encounter. Typically they will both attack the same opponent, trying to down each foe in turn. They retreat from fire if strongly presented, and are intelligent enough to avoid heavily armored foes if offered a "softer" target.

Worg: HD 4; AC 6[13]; Atk 1 bite (1d6+1); Move 18; Save 13; CL/XP 4/120; Special: None.

8-9 Herd Animals. A herd of deer, elk or otherwise innocuous beasts is spooked by the characters and runs by. Fast thinking players can shoot arrows and get a few free meals (assume each animal is AC 7[12] and has 2d6 hp).

10. Trap. One thing about woods that have kobolds in them, is that they often are filled with traps. These little devils have constructed several traps in this area. Roll randomly to determine the type:

1d6	Trap
1	Pit trap, 10 feet deep (1d6 damage), save avoids
2	Log swings down (save avoids) hitting all within its path for 1d6+1 damage
3	Foot snare catches a random character, save avoids being swung up into a tree or other hard surface for 1d6 damage and being left hanging by one's leg, 10 feet in the air.
4	Javelin trap attacks a random character as a 4 HD monster for 1d6 damage
5	Pungi sticks, a 3 foot deep pit full of spikes, save or fall in for 2d6 damage.
6	Swinging bees nest trap, This is treated as if an insect plague spell had been cast, centered on a random player character.

11. Crazy old person. A VERY unstable and dangerous madman who is initially encountered singing softly to him/herself. This madman seems harmless until the characters bed down or are otherwise unawares. The madman then attacks with ferocity (treat as a berserker). This encounter only occurs once.

Crazy Old Person: HD 1; AC 7[12]; Atk 1 weapon (1d8); Move 12; Save 17; CL/XP 2/30; Special: +2 to hit in berserk state; Gear: Odd implements.

12. Owlbear. This horrific creature plows through trees and brush to get at its victims. A clever tracker can find its lair (a small cave). The lair contains the remains of a fighter (platemail, longsword and 23 gp in a pouch).

Owlbear: HD 5+1; AC 5[14]; Atk 2 claws (1d6) and 1 bite (2d6); Move 12; Save 12; CL/XP 5/240; Special: Hug for an additional 2d8 damage if to-hit roll 18+.

1. Fog. Fog has settled in during the night. Being on watch consists of straining to see further than twenty feet in any direction. It seems the croak of frogs and the swish of passing crocodiles and snakes are just outside of your visible range. A sudden flurry of wings erupts a short distance from the camp, quickly followed by the frustrated cry of a swamp cougar. The swamp's nightlife seems to be happening all around you, but characters cannot see any of it.

2-4. Crocodile. A crocodile stalks the characters. It attacks any that enter the water (or automatically if it surprises). If it kills someone, it grabs the body and retreats to deep water immediately.

Crocodile: HD 3; AC 4[15]; Atk 1 bite (1d6); Move 9 (Swim 12); Save 14; CL/XP 3/60; Special: None.

5. Grey Ooze. Anyone who has seen a blob movie knows how this one goes. The ooze retreats into the water if dropped to 1/2 HPs. Otherwise it attacks mindlessly.

Grey Ooze: HD 3; AC 8[11]; Atk 1 strike (2d6); Move 1; Save 14; CL/XP 5/240; Special: Acid (metal and wood touching it must save [12] or be rotted through), immune to: spells, head, cold, and blunt weapons.

6. Quicksand. A random character falls into quicksand. This is not particularly hazardous as long as they are not alone, or in heavy armor. Light armored characters can free themselves if they make a save. There is no save for anyone in anything heavier than leather armor. Anyone trapped sinks in rounds equal to their base (not including dexterity or magic) armor class unless pulled free by someone outside of the quicksand. Anyone pulled under dies in 3 rounds after immersion.

7. Giant Beaver. This large animal is not dangerous as long as they are left alone. Encounters can range from having the characters "trespass" on the beaver's territory (and dam) to randomly encountering one chewing down a tree. If the characters back off, the beaver will do the same. Beavers are territorial; however, if anyone can speak with animals, they can be friendly to a group as long as no threat is perceived. The safety of a giant beaver dam could be a wonderful hiding spot/campsite if the beaver is befriended or slain.

Giant Beaver: HD 3; AC 6[13]; Atk 1 bite (1d6) and 1 tail slap (1d6); Move 9 (Swim 12); Save 14; CL/XP 3/60; Special: None.

8-9. Herd Animals. A herd of deer, elk or otherwise innocuous beasts is spooked by the characters and runs by. Fast thinking players can shoot arrows and get a few free meals (assume each animal is AC 7[12] and has 2d6 hp).

10. Ghouls (1d3). These creatures are encountered mostly at night, although daytime encounters are possible. They haunt the swamp looking for flesh to eat; preferably human flesh.

Ghoul: HD 2; AC 6[13]; Atk 2 claws (1d3 + paralyze) and 1 bite (1d4 + paralyze); Move 9; Save 16; CL/XP 3/50; Special: Immune to sleep and charm, paralyzing touch for 3d6 turns (save avoids).

11.Giant Constrictor Snake. Preying even on small crocodiles, the valley is home to large pythons that act as the local apex predator (excepting the dragon). These snakes typically do not attack anything during the day, preferring to sleep in the large trees that make up their nests. A typical encounter would be for a sleeping character to be attacked (surprise at night is 1-5/6). Anyone bitten and squeezed while asleep cannot make a sound if they are dropped below 0 hp (and killed). The snakes typically retreat if wounded more than 50% of their hp.

Giant Constrictor Snake: HD 6; AC 5[14]; Atk 1 bite (1d3) and 1 constrict (2d4); Move 10; Save 11; CL/XP 7/600; Special: Constrict (do automatic damage after hitting, 1 in 6 chance of pinning an arm or leg).

12. Sub-Adult Black Dragon. Living in the swamp is Recaltrix the dragon. She is a fine swimmer, and prefers to come out of the swamp (posing as a crocodile) to flying (due to the heavy tree cover). Recaltrix is almost cat-like in her hunting techniques, and prefers to watch her prey and attack when it suits her.

Recaltrix, Black Dragon: HD 6; HP: 18; AC 2[17]; Atk 2 claws (1d4) and 1 bite (3d6); Move 9 (Fly 24, Swim 12); Save 11; CL/XP 8/800; Special: Spits acid (18 damage).

Keyed Encounter Areas

1. The Black Spire

As the characters journey through the lush green land they see ahead a round grassy mound with a slender finger of stone at its top. When they approach, you can see the hill is about twenty feet high and forty feet across at the base. Atop this mound is a granite obelisk seven feet high. [Should someone climb the mound to examine the obelisk:] The stone is old and weather worn, with an inscription at its base written in a forgotten script. Behind the obelisk is a large patch of freshly turned earth.

Against the horizon is a tall, black spire. It stands about fifteen feet tall, its surface beaten and cracked by weather. There are marks all over the surface, but too much time has passed since they were carved, and they are now just shallow tracings in the stone. If the adventurers try to read the marks, they will realize the carvings are in an ancient tongue that they cannot read. The obelisk is merely a border marker of an empire that fell long ago.

2. Empty Armor

Lying beside the road is a set of leather armor. A full torso of tiny leather plates sewn together lies on the grass, still in a round shape with the straps closed, so it gives the eerie impression of still being worn, even though the wearer cannot be seen. The owner must have been a middle-sized man, quite broad-shouldered. If the area is searched, they find the leg armor scattered in the grass, dispelling the illusion that anyone is in the body armor. No helm, weapons pack or shoes can be found, only leather armor. The armor is still supple and soft, although in some places grass is growing up through it. Grass grows fast and leather weathers quickly, so this cannot have been here long.

3. The Bandit Camp

There is an odd structure up ahead, instantly distinguished by straight lines in an environment where all things curve. As the characters near the structure they can determine that it is the wall of an old building. Two sides still stand but the grassland has reclaimed all the area around the walls. The two walls, only a story high, are at right angles to each other and protrude awkwardly out of the plain. On the one facing you, part of the interior when the building was complete, you are struck by reflections off an old mosaic that covers the wall. The tiles are still bright blue and white. Despite the gaps from missing tiles, you recognize the scene as a mountain above a blue lake. No real mountains or lakes are visible anywhere. Living here are 3 bandits, there is a 50% chance that one is on guard, giving a 1-3/6 chance of surprise.

Bandit 1—armed with a shortbow, 8 arrows and a spear (0 Level Human, AC 6[13], 6 hp). Wears leather armor and carries a wooden shield. He has a belt pouch with a lump of translucent amber wax the size of an apricot (5 cp) and something reddish glistens inside. Prying the wax ball open, you discover a jagged piece of pink rhodochrosite (9 gp) the size of a child's thumbnail.

Bandit 2—armed with a 3 throwing axes and shortsword, and wears studded leather armor (0 Level Human, AC 6[13], 7 hp). This bandit has a small sack on his belt containing pair of beeswax candles (1 cp each), perfumed with lavender, have been jammed carelessly into a pocket. The candles were originally shaped like dancing girls, but as they have burned down, the wax has deformed the 'dancers' strangely. Only the legs and hips remain clearly defined.

Bandit 3—armed with a shortbow, 12 arrows, and a greatsword, and wears studded leather armor (0 Level Human, AC 6[13], 6 hp). In his pouch are three gold coins, a round wooden box full of a fragrant yellow wax (mustache wax, 2 gp) and a bright woven ribbon, red, purple and white, made of some fine material (silk) about as long as one arm but thinner than your little fingernail.

Tactics: The bandits will not openly engage a larger party if they have surprise, but instead spread out in the brush and attack from all sides with missiles, targeting lightly armored foes first. They run if one of them is slain.

Treasure: In the camp are 4 boxes of foodstuffs (20 days rations), a small keg of wine (worth 10 gp), bedrolls, a tinderbox, 4 flasks of lamp oil and a lantern. A sack of 60 tallow candles hangs from a hook on one wall. In one bedroll is a pouch containing a set of dice and 36 sp. Stretched between two poles are the partially tanned hides of three deer and a beaver (worth 1 gp each for the deer hides and 4 gp for the beaver pelt). Wedged into one of the poles is a hide scraper (worth 2 gp), and at the base is a pot of oily wax (worth 10 sp) used in tanning hides. A pile of firewood rests against another wall, and a chopping axe lays on top of it.

4. An Empty Burrow

Concealed amongst the tall grass is a large, flat boulder. Below the front edge someone or something has burrowed under the rock, creating a small shelter. (The burrow is small and dark, but big enough for a person of average size to squeeze inside. If someone looks inside, or enters:) The small space is damp and smells strongly of wet fur. There are scatterings of bird bones and small piles of dried dung littering the floor. There is no other life in here except for a few beetles, crawling slowly along the wall. A ceramic drinking mug decorated with a rose quartz (11 gp) is filled with torn paper lies on the floor. Mixed in the dirt near the mug is an assortment of 25 silver temple coins, stamped with the faces of saints (worth 25 gp). At the bottom of the mug, is a golden sphere the size of a die (15 gp). The wadded torn up fragments of paper, each bear strange writing in deep indigo ink. This is the remains of a scroll of the arcane spell suggestion. Amazingly, none of the tears broke any of the lettering, so if the scroll is repaired, or if the pieces are carefully laid out, it can still be used.

5. For the Want of an Axle...

Nestled in the tall grass is a broken-down wagon. The peeling paint on the wind-blasted sideboards reads 'Mygo's's Traveling Mystical Emporium.' The rear axle is broken, causing the wagon to sag drunkenly to the left. The leather harnesses are rotting away, still connected to the shaft. The tattered canvas cover has been destroyed leaving the metal frame highlighted against the sky like the ribs of some great beast. The wheels have sunken into the prairie ground several inches. It would seem that the wagon was abandoned long ago. A heavy woolen cloak (14 gp), dyed dark blue, lies crumpled in a corner. Lighter blue ink has been used to trace wandering spiral patterns on the cloak, and the fine garment's edges have been trimmed in bone-white thread and feathers. A silver clasp in the shape of a walrus is used to secure the cloak (36 gp). (Total 50 gp). The right interior pocket holds a leather scroll case. Within the leather scroll case are three sheets of plain parchment scribed in a utilitarian, easy-to-read script. Each sheet is labeled "Protection for the traveling wizard" in the Common tongue. Each of the scrolls is identical, and bears a casting of the spell shield. The thick leather scroll case has been repeatedly treated with waterproof and flame proofing oils. It weighs one pound and is worth 50 gp.

6. The Ogre Cave

If encountered at night, a dim light can be seen coming from a cave entrance on the side of a steep cliff. If encountered in day, several dozen bones and skulls can be seen at the base of the cliff below the cave entrance, with an area of brown, dead vegetation along the cliff face.

The cave itself sits on the edge of a 40-foot cliff along the trail winding down into the valley. The trail itself is approximately 20 feet wide, with a sand-crumbly edge being held together by vegetation. The entrance is 10 feet wide and 7 feet high, and is obscured with brambles and vines tacked onto a crossbar set of tree limbs. The vines are dead (unlike the rest of the vegetation on the hillside, and one doesn't have to be an elf to notice that this is probably a (poorly) concealed door.

The concealed door (the wood and vines) is hung with 4 large brass bells on the back side that are hung to clink and ring with a considerable echo if the door is handled roughly. Careful examination of the false door (rather than just tossing it aside) reveals the bells and can prevent the Ogre and his pet bear from immediately knowing they have company.

Beyond the door is a cave tunnel widening to 20 feet wide and 12 feet high, branching of to the left and right sides at the 30 foot mark. The floor of the cave is course, tan sand, and broken stalactites and stalagmites (obviously broken intentionally) litter the floor. Remains of a campfire freshly doused with water (daytime) or a small coal fire (at night) is immediately inside the doorway.

6A. The Pantry and Spring

The left tunnel leads to a 40-foot diameter dead-end cave containing a 10-foot diameter pool of clean, clear water. The pool is 8 feet deep and flows through cracks in the walls of the pool in both directions, providing an excellent and replenishing water source. Many small, blind crayfish crawl around the pool.

Hanging from the walls of the cave are three gutted dear, one stretched wolf pelt, and one dead (and gutted and dressed) human. Blood stains the sand near the hanging corpses, and flies and small cave beetles have been attracted to the remains.

Note that is the bell trap was sounded, and the characters went this way first, it is highly likely that they are attacked from the rear after 1d4 rounds.

MCMLXXV
Wilderness

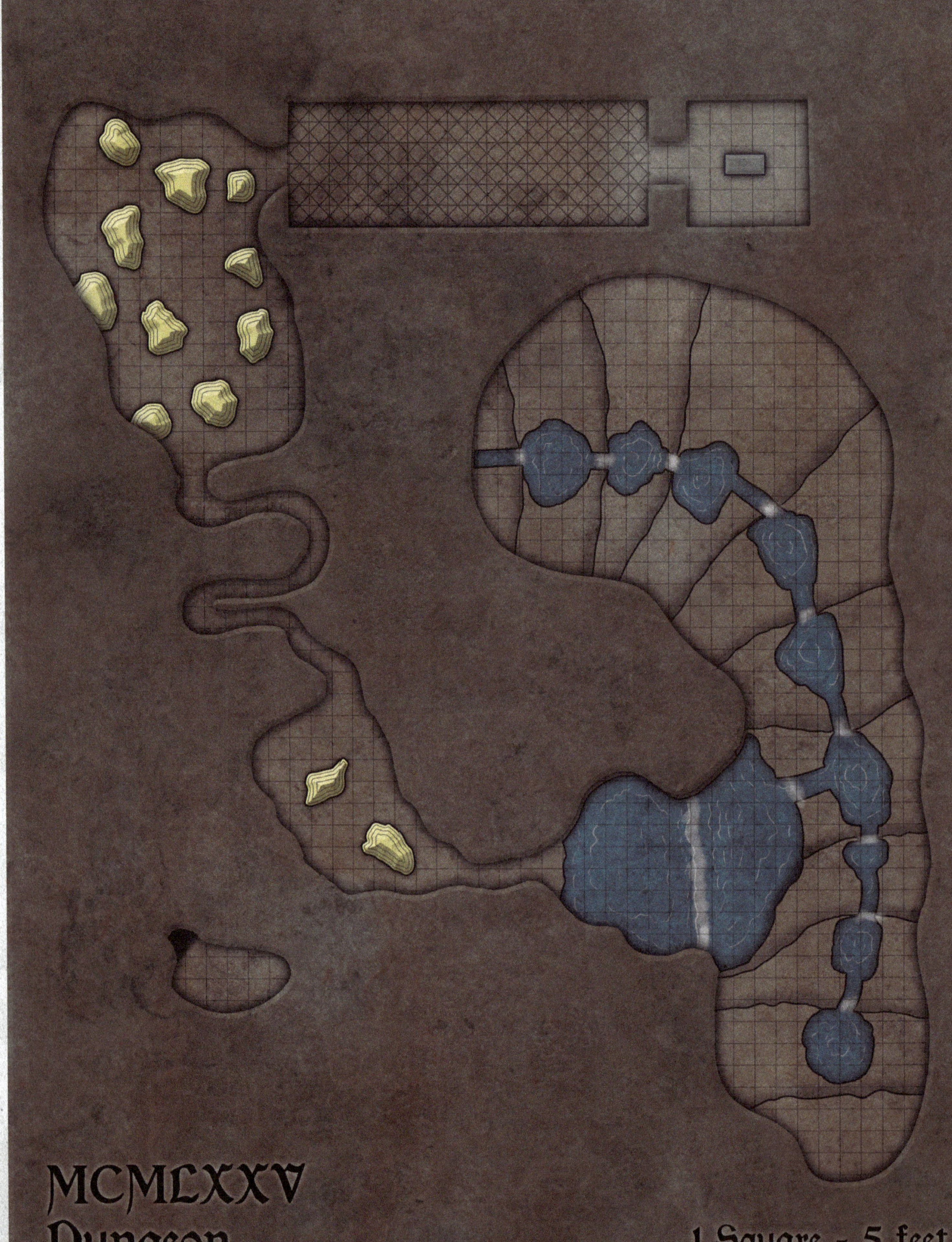

MCMLXXV
Dungeon
1 Square - 5 feet

MCMLXXV
Wilderness
Town
1
2
3
4
5
6
7
8
9
10
11
12
13
14
15
16
17
18
19
20
21
22
23
24
25
26
27

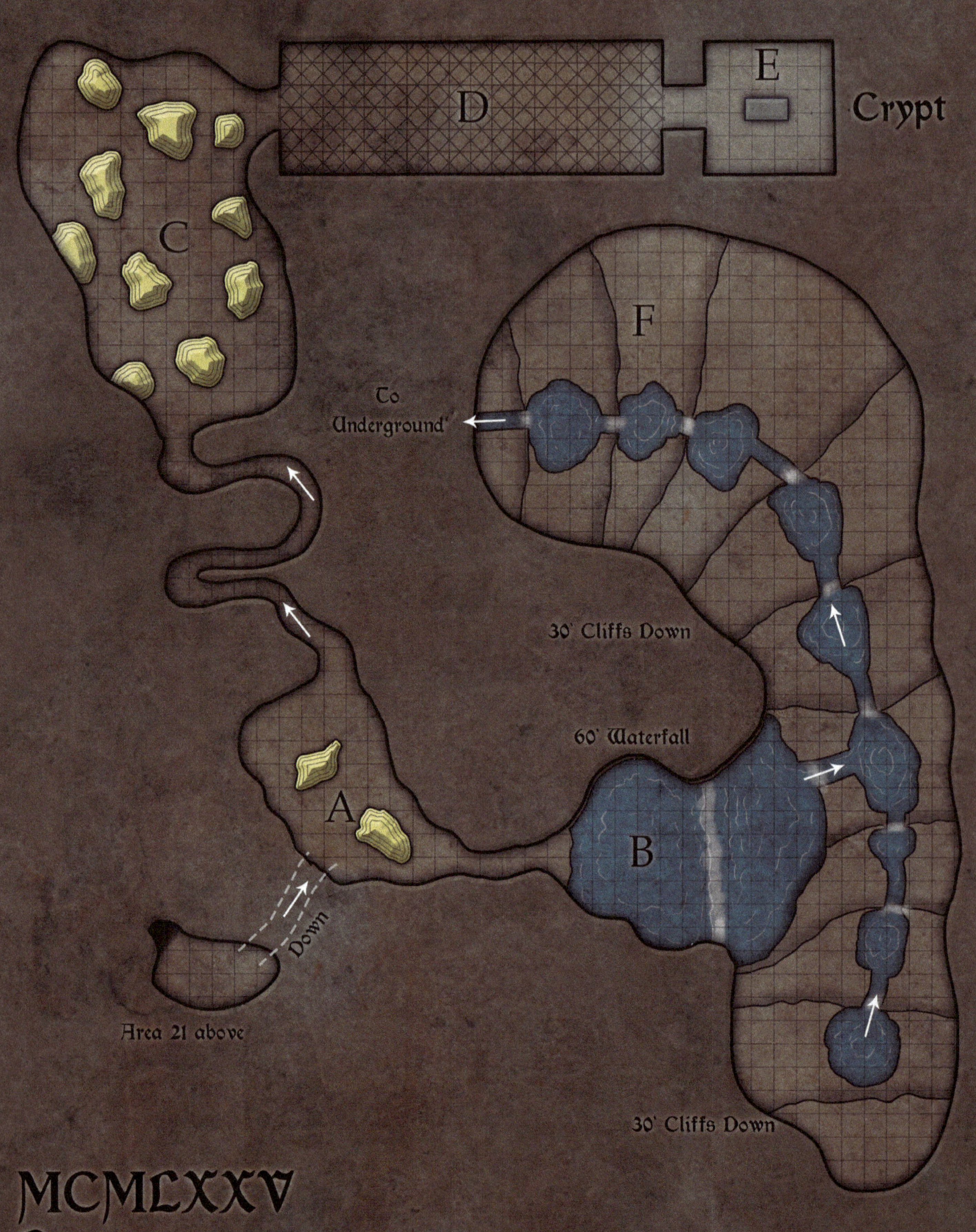
D
E
Crypt
C
F
To Underground
30' Cliffs Down
60' Waterfall
A
B
Down
Area 21 above
30' Cliffs Down
MCMLXXV
Dungeon
1 Square - 5 feet

6B. THE OGRE'S DEN

The right tunnel leads back 80 feet to a 50 foot long, 30 foot wide chamber. The cave smells foul, like sweat and filth of some sort. The ceiling is fully 12 feet high, and has had all the lime deposits knocked down (the ogre was tired of hitting his head on them). A large pile of rubble lines the back wall of the cave, obscuring the ogre's nest (see below). A huge pile of firewood is stacked against the left wall, and a fire pit made of stacked rocks rests in the center of the cave, complete with a cooking spit and a large pot. The ceiling is well ventilated, and bats flitter about the roof (and leave the cave via small cracks in the roof.

Unless the players have been very stealthy, the Ogre and his pet black bear are here and ready for combat. They fight to the death if encountered in the cave (there is no retreat). If one speaks ogre, it is also possible to parley with them, although the Ogre thinks of any intrusion into his home as burglary as a starting point for the negotiations. The pair will not pursue a large group outside of the cave.

The Ogre: HD 4+1; HP 22; AC 4[15] (he is wearing heavy furs); Atk 1 club (1d10+1); Move 9; Save 13; AL C; CL/XP 4/120; Special: None.
Black Bear: HD 4+1; AC 7[12]; Atk 2 claws (1d3), 1 bite (1d6); Move 9; Save 13; AL N; CL/XP 4/120; Special: Hug (1d8).

The Ogre's nest is a foul collection of torn bedding and soiled clothing, most of it shredded into long, worthless strips. The hilt of a greatsword pokes out from beneath the pile. It is in decent condition, if a bit rusty. Next to the sword is a suit of worn but serviceable banded mail (AC 4[15]) sized for a large human or half-orc. A few bones are still lying near the banded mail, and they show evidence of having been gnawed on. A backpack lies by the armor; like the bedding, it has been shredded to worthlessness. Its contents lie strewn throughout the pile. The remains of trail rations are mixed with a destroyed pile of rope and scraps from a canvas sack. Several dozen coins are scattered amongst the refuse (69 gp, 148 sp). Buried in the back is a shortbow which, surprisingly, shows no wear save for a missing bowstring. A quiver of arrows is here as well, chewed through, but still containing three silver arrows.

Next to the bedding is a latched chest (with a **poison needle** trap), a bucket and a bow. A longbow of yew with a grip of pale calfskin (75 gp) lies beside a quiver of deer hide tooled all over with cleverly intertwined hunting scenes (5 gp). There are no arrows in the quiver but it holds a silver flask (etched with flower decorations) which is full of rich red wine (flask 10 gp; wine 1 gp). The chest contains a light leather riding saddle (10 gp), a square of fine lace (5 gp) and a pair of white elbow-length gloves sprinkled with freshwater pearls around the top (pair 340 gp). Beside them, wrapped in a rag, is a stick of charcoal and a 3-inch diameter crystal sphere. A tall thin book with poorly executed carving on its wooden covers is half-full of amateur sketches of people and animals, done in charcoal (5 sp). Caught in a seam at the bottom is a red-brown garnet (100 gp).

The heavy, solid brass bucket (2 gp) holds two fine silver platters (30 gp each), a black stone cat with yellow eyes (onyx with 2 small citrines; 250 gp), a hinged box with a tiny hunting scene on the top in bright enamels (15 gp) and a heavy coin pouch. The little box holds a fine powder (one-half pound cinnamon, 5 sp; or a spell component or other spice). In the coin pouch are 65 gp, 393 sp, 203 cp and 3 pieces of turquoise (10 gp each).

Polished to a mirror-like sheen, this smooth sphere of clear crystal is surprisingly heavy, and is about the size of a plum. The sphere erupts in bright silver light that clearly illuminates the area around. When held in hand, this crystal sphere radiates silver light brightly out to 20 feet, and dimly out to 40 feet. The sphere automatically activates when grasped, and deactivates one round after being released.

7. RIVER CROSSING

The path is split by a deep chasm with a river at the bottom. There is a bridge across it, made of a single log. A big tree has been cut and dropped over the chasm. There is no other way across except to walk on the tree. The tree was more than a hundred feet tall and at least sixty of those feet are out over the chasm. Below is a river with rushing white water between tall boulders. The bark is still on this tree bridge but the branches have been chopped off. A slightly lighter color down the center shows the path. It's about a foot wide and level. On both sides another six inches of log slopes away. It's not a difficult path, if you don't mind being suspended in space sixty feet above a wild river.

8. RUINED COTTAGE

The trail winds over a dark sandy soil, comfortable to walk or ride on because it gives slightly but makes little dust. The temperature is pleasant in the shade of the great trees. The air carries sweet plant scents (such as pine and wintergreen). In all directions are tall broad-leafed trees, or really, their trunks, reaching upward. Occasionally the trunks are those of pines, leaking sticky, fragrant sap. Middle-sized shrubs dot the forest floor. Between them are ferns and grasses but most of the ground is bare except for fallen, brown leaves and fuzzy deep green mosses. A ruined building ahead makes a stark contrast. Only one wall stands, but one can see a dark empty area where the interior was, and sections of the fallen walls are visible. In front weeds, rare here in the forest, form a wild tangle of green and brown shoots. It is both forlorn and ugly. Four transparent glass bottles are lined up side by side on a small shelf inside the remains. Each is large enough to contain perhaps a pint of liquid and is stoppered by a substantial cork. Each has a fairly thick liquid in which different items of food are packed. The first contains pickled garlic bulbs, the second pickled eggs of some sort, perhaps hens' eggs, the third, strands of red cabbage and the final one has small, silvery fish. In the bottom of the fish bottle are also 4 silvery coins (40 gp).

9. SPIDERS AND FLIES

What began as the occasional spider web has now quickly blossomed into gossamer curtains and sheets of webbing. There is evidence that the webs have been hacked and burned away from the trail, but the forest has web upon web. All around is the smell dust and decay. Here and there, you see hanging objects that could be bodies; too many of them seem to be humanoid in shape. Everywhere you look, you see gleams that seem to be glittering eyes staring back at you. Eerily, you notice that you can no longer hear the normal sounds of the forest – only the gentle sighing of a mournful wind. Six large spiders, and one huge spider lurk in the trees. Each round 1d3-1 spiders notice the party and stalk them, attacking once 3 or more spiders have seen them. Large spiders are 1+1 HD, hp 4 each, AC 8[11], Move 6"/15", damage 1+ poison (save at +2 or incapacitated in 1d3 round. The Huge spider is 2+2 HD, hp 12, AC 6[13], Move 6"/15", damage 1d6+ poison save at +1 or incapacitated in 1 round. One of the corpses has a sack. In a sack (1 sp) you find a large, half-burned yellow candle (3 cp), two thin gray blankets (wool, 2 sp ea), a heavy black skillet (iron, 2 sp), an old, large wooden spoon (2 cp), a mink pelt (20 gp), a rabbit pelt (2 gp), and a black leather belt, carefully made with inconspicuous, very fine tooling along its length. However, the buckle is missing and was very sloppily cut off (3 gp). The sack also holds a coil of coarse rope (1 gp), a pair of gauntlets of heavy cowhide dyed black, held by solid iron rivets reworked to look like stars (5 gp), and a silver key (1 gp). Loose at the bottom are various coins and black and white stones. (7 gp, 19 sp, 33 cp; 2 pieces of obsidian 10 gp each; 1 small piece of onyx, 20 gp; 2 pieces of quartz 10 gp each) (Total 101.98 gp). Also present is a club hewn from a gnarled oaken limb, preserved with a dark finish. The large burl of wood at the business end has been stained a dark, rusty red from repeated use. The grip is bound in strips of cream-colored leather bearing fine runes dyed into the material. The leather strips can be unwrapped from the club to reveal two castings of the druid spell warp wood. Each strip is four inches wide and two feet long. Though not masterwork, the three-pound club is quite serviceable.

10. Mysterious Shrine

Next to the path but partially hidden by a screen of smaller plants, a small shrine composed of stacked rocks and twigs has been established around a crudely carved 3 foot statue . The statue has chubby arms and legs and a welcoming smile, together with some tiny clay bowls and plates. Bits of food and drink have been set in front of the god as a form of tribute. A small scorched area perhaps indicates where a fire has been set, although it may have been nothing more than a large candle.

11. A Fork in the Road

The ground surrounding the path here is completely blanketed with a vibrant, blue clover, the bright full blooms almost glowing in the gloom of the woods. Hovering and darting above the clover are tiny white butterflies. There is a rustling among the clover and a small green viper courses his way through the plants. Careful inspection reveals a glimpse of something gleaming dully among the greenery. If the adventurers search through the clover, they discover a small pewter skeleton key, the top of which is carved to resemble a squat little face of a mouse with a protruding tongue. There is a 10% chance that the little viper, which slithers quickly from the clover bed and across the path, is disturbed by the party and attacks.

Viper: HD 1d6 hp; AC 5[14]; Atk 1 bite (1 + poison); Move 18; Save 18; CL/XP 2/30; Special: Lethal poison (save at +2 or die).

12. Mushrooms and Fishhooks

Here the trees are spaced more widely apart and more sunlight reaches the forest floor. Some of the trees are ancient, reaching heights of a hundred feet or more and spanning 10 to 15 feet across. The trees' great, twisted roots have grown over the trail in many places, at times rising four feet above the ground before delving back into the loamy earth. Dozens of tiny red mushrooms sprout from the soft wood of the roots, creating a strange almost anthill-like appearance. Along in the trail, two of the enormous trees have grown toward each other, their great roots intertwining and forming a latticework wall that completely bars the path.

At the blocked section, the roots have grown in a way that suggests a ladder, easy to climb despite the slippery nature of the moss and the mushrooms growing on them. The roots go up about eight feet. If any of the party climb them, they find a small 'nest' of twigs and leaves tucked up against the trunk of one great tree. It is about the right size for a creature two feet tall. It contains a dirty suit of clothes in a very small size, a tiny pair of shoes, and a small locked iron box. (If any of the party has the skeleton key above, it will fit into the keyhole and can be used to unlock the box.) Inside is arrayed rows of fish hooks in different sizes and materials. The smallest would be suitable for landing minnows while some of the larger ones would probably be strong enough to cope with a particularly fierce shark. Some of the smaller hooks are fashioned from stone and some kind of crystal, while the larger ones are made from some kind of steel (80 hooks, 50 gp). If anyone steals the hooks, Jasper the Leprechaun that owns them will become very upset.

Leprechaun: HD 1; AC 8[11]; Atk 1 weapon (1d6); Move 18; Save 15; CL/XP 5/240; Special: Magic resistance 10%, spell abilities - at will: dimension door, invisibility; 1/day: phantasmal force

The little fellow hides invisibly high in a tree, and does not bother the party unless his abode is disturbed. Should the group leave food (or wine), Jasper might be favorably disposed towards them, even helping them in their next fight, although he still will not reveal himself. He will instead use his polymorph ability to transform opponent's swords into mushrooms and the like. If the hooks are stolen by the party, the opposite is true. The little fellow plagues the group with untied shoelaces, spoiled food, misplaced items and turns a sword into a snake when the group is in combat. The Referee can use his imagination to create havoc as desired.

If a great quantity of wine or spirits is left as an offering, the party has an opportunity to capture Jasper. Like all his kind, he has a propensity to indulge a bit heavily when given the opportunity. While he remains invisible, the drunk leprechaun can be located by his loud snoring. If captured, Jasper offers his pot of gold (400 gp) for his freedom. The gold is buried on a small hill not far from the tree lattice.

13. Into the Swamp

At the edge of a thickly forested territory, the players marvel at the new plant life all around, and feel water begin to creep into their boots. Anyone looking down notices that the forest floor ahead is flooded. The swamp ahead is alive with new growth; yellow birch trees with new catkins (flowers) hanging from the branches, and the dark green scale-like leaves of white cedar trees. They also notice the intense smells all around. Some enticing aromas come from new flowers blooming above the water, but others are not so appealing, like the smell of fetid leaves still decaying from last year's fall season. One cannot see very far ahead into the swamp due to the overgrowth of the trees (vision limited to 90 feet in the swamp).

13. Wet Feet

The path descends into the dark waters of the swamp. Tall grasses grow up in the shallows where the path should be, and sections of the trail are underwater. The murky waters swirl sluggishly and ripples indicate something large swimming across the road just below the surface. Ahead the path rises out of the water and continues on. If the adventurers follow the path they will find that the water covering it is waist deep. Anyone who misses a dexterity check could slip and fall. The Referee should decide if there is a risk of an encounter. Also, if the adventurers move to the right or left of the road the water quickly rises to neck deep.

14. Rats!

A plump, insolent-looking rat sits on the matted moss on top of a dead stump in the water at the side of the trail and licks its lips suggestively. It waits there, daring anyone to throw a stone, which it might well ignore. The water bubbles around the rat and a burst of foul-smelling gas suddenly fills the air. The rat looks like it is smirking. Long white whiskers stand out against its grey, well-groomed fur. Green eyes gleam in what remains of the daylight and they have a look of intelligence far greater than any rat should have. If attacked, the rat can easily be slain (1 hp, AC 6[13]). A better idea would be to toss it something shiny.

The rat's nest is a few yards into the swamp, just off the trail. In its nest are several items. For some reason, this rat feels a need to "trade" shiny objects from time to time. Should the characters toss it an object, it runs off and returns with an exchange gift. It will do this up to three times. What the rat brings back is randomly determined, but can include:

1. A silver piece
2. A gold piece
3. A small gem (10 gp)
4. A worthless polished rock
5. A broken piece of china or glass
6. A large white tooth (of a crocodile or other beast)
7. A small mirror made of silver (15 gp)
8. A magical +1 ring of protection

Items 7 and 8 can only be gotten once.

15. Bubble Spit and Chomp

The swamp bubbles and spits, methane deposits just under the water exploding rhythmically. The air is so humid and close that it's hard to breathe. In the water is a crocodile (3 HD, 19 hp, AC 5[14], Move 6"/24", damage 2-8 (tail) and 1-12 (bite). It surprises on a 1-3/6 normally, although this one is on the opposite shore, and resting, having eaten recently, and only attacks if someone enters the water. If the party comes back this way again, the crocodile may be hungry (50% chance), and lying in ambush near the water's edge.

16. Just Chomp

Here the swamp forest forms a gallery overhead. Great trees with air plants dangling from them arch over the swamp. The water is so still one can see their reflection in its dark surface. The tree trunks are gray or occasionally light brown, thin and smooth. Most are quite plain, but a few are twisted round and round with climbing vines. They branch far overhead, but the limbs are long and bend down to dip leaves in the water. A bright red and white butterfly basks on an olive green leaf near the water's edge, its wings flicking slowly up and down. In the water is a crocodile (3 HD, 15 hp, AC 5[14], Move 6"/24", damage 2-8 (tail) and 1-12 (bite). It surprises on a 1-3/6, and attacks anyone within 10 feet of the trails edge.

17. The Island of Screams

About 30 feet through chest deep water is a 40-foot diameter island, rising up out of the swamp. This portion of the bog smells of rot, decay, and fermenting wood. Every place where the ground rises up out of the water is speckled with tiny white and tan mushrooms. Fallen logs lay soaked and decomposing all around, most of them covered with broader, slimy looking fungus and moss.

The trees on the island that are still standing are ringed with brown shelf-like fungi in tiers around their trunks. The mushrooms are getting larger the further onto the island. I the center of the island is a small area where they seem to have replaced the trees entirely. About a half-dozen of the fungi are tall enough that the caps are spread above the character's heads and there's a fine mist of yellowish green spores sprinkling down from each. Beyond these few large ones, the mushrooms gradually get smaller again. These large mushrooms include 3 Shriekers (3 HD, 14 hp, AC 7[12], Shriek if approached within 5 feet—attracts wandering monsters 50% chance).

If a monster is indicated, in this case it's a troll, 6+6 HD, 30 hp, AC 4[15], damage 5-8 x 2 and 2-12, regenerates). The troll carries a sack. A large heavy sack contains a length of fine brown silk (3 yards, 30 gp), a plain gold cup too small for a halfling to get a good drink (25 gp) and a large piece of carved white rock. The carving is two hands long and is the head of a man with an aquiline nose and thinning hair. It was obviously broken off from a larger sculpture. There's also an iron mace studded with pointed spikes longer than a finger. A ball of thick white yarn (1 gp) has tangled all around the mace and its spikes. There's also a small shiny round metal cylinder with a cap that holds toothpicks (cylinder silver 5 gp, toothpicks 1 cp). Scattered across the bottom are coins and 2 pale blue gems, (19 sp, 25 cp, and 2 pieces of blue quartz, 10 gp each).

18. A Really Big Tree

Even among the towering trees in this swamp, this one is huge. If a group of six held hands they still might not be able to reach around its base. The bark is weathered and dark, with odd cracks and crevices. In places the bark has come off and the rich red-brown wood can be seen. On this side, along the trail, the great tree is on land, but the other side of the immense trunk is surrounded by green swamp water. The branches, some bigger than many individual trees, spread far overhead. At the tree's base is what must be a forest altar of some sort, fresh flowers are lying there, atop older dry flowers and unidentifiable items. A large granite boulder lies ahead, the path snaking around it.

Past granite boulder, the size of a small mountain, is a colorful sight. A field full of vibrant flowers, of every shape and size, dances to the tune of the breeze. Floral scents fill the character's nostrils, along with the tickle of pollen. The soft trickling sound of a stream nearby makes this an almost serene place. It appears initially that they have exited the swamp; however another step proves this wrong, as their feet foot submerge into the cold and inundated soil. (A rare find indeed, as normally flowers like the ones mentioned above do not abide in swamps. There may, however there may be a special reason behind this, it's possibly the domicile of a swamp druid, or perhaps the soil here is just perfect for this type of plant life.)

Gnarled, pungent vines grow out of deep cracks in the head of an ancient statue. Taller than a grown man, it lies upside down in the oily muck, only the base of its nose and its snarling lips visible above the scum of dead leaves and still water. The statue must have once been painted striking greens and yellows and reds, but age has reduced its brilliant colors to pastels. The roots of a twisted river oak grow in thick tangles around the severed head. Some distance away lies an enormous hand, missing half its fingers, which is now home to a nest of water moccasins. The snakes are highly aggressive, and attack if disturbed, with 1d4 of them joining combat each round until all are slain or the characters retreat more than 60 feet from the statue. Of the rest of the forgotten statue, there is no sign.

Water Moccasin (12): HD 1d6 hp; AC 5[14]; Atk 1 bite (1 + poison); Move 18 (Swim 12); Save 18; CL/XP 2/30; Special: Lethal poison (save at +4 or die).

19. The Pond

The trail vanishes into a pond here. Circling along the edge, looking for the trail, branches slap at your faces and your gear (such as packs or protruding weapons) gets caught by vines. The pond appears to be at least 100 feet across, but its edge is irregular and not easy to see. At the far edge, at what ought to be the pond's exit, is a beaver dam. The dam is woven of logs, sticks and leaves, easily six feet high above the stream at its center, three feet at its edges. It is in excellent repair; some of the branches on it still have green leaves. The pond spreads out from there and one can see the top of a beaver lodge 20 yards out in the pond. The stream spills under the dam, filling a wide channel there. The pond covers the trail. The players have to pick a place to ford the stream, either above or below the dam. The trail continues once the pond is crossed or river forded. Curiously, there is no beaver.

Several small turtles, mostly a hand span across but sometimes larger or smaller, can be seen in the pond. Most are scrunched together on a log a dozen yards out in the center of the pond and around the beaver lodge. They bask in a strange posture in the occasional beam of sunlight, their heads and legs all sticking stiffly out from the shell.. A giant turtle hides in the pond. Anyone at the ponds edge for more than 3 rounds will likely be surprised and attacked. The turtle has 5 HD, 22 HP, AC 0[19] (shell)/5[14] (neck and head), moves 3"/4" (in water) and does 3-12 damage on a bite. It surprises on a 1-4/6 if attacking while submerged.

20. Narrow Path, Big Pig

The path travels alongside a stream for a space, and rises up out of the mud a few feet, creating a ledge down to the water of about 8 feet. Although the trail is clear and the stream is obvious, the plants along the stream edge are very dense and difficult to move through.

Along the ridge, a female wild boar noses for grubs before a gently swaying wall of cattails. Six piglets nose along the ground, their snouts and stubby, immature tusks covered in rich brown mud. They oink happily, till the mother catches sight of the party. She stands her ground, grunting angrily, as her young barrel into the thicket. As soon as they are out of sight, she joins them, knocking over cattails in her haste to get to safety. If the group does not retreat in 3 rounds, she attacks (3+3 HD, Move 12", hp 19, AC 7[12], damage 3-12, fight to -7). The only way around her is to swim or wade through the water below.

21. St. Elmo

Each step causes a sucking sound from the bottom of the character's boots as they release from the muck. Ahead is unusually large tree. It is vacant of all its leaves, and its branches reach out like arms in towards the group. The dark gray lines that run vertically through its pasty white trunk seem somehow to form a face. A large knot protruding from the center of the tree resembles a nose, while a hollowed opening under the knot reminds has the appearance of a mouth. A slowly pulsating, yellowish light escapes this hole, reminiscent of a firefly in the distance and dances off into the trees. The glowing light is a highly dangerous Will-o-the-Wisp, and is far beyond the abilities of the group. It is 9 HD, 44 hp, AC -8[27], damage 2-16, and immune to all spells except protection from evil, magic missile and maze. It will not attack unless attacked, but instead will try to draw the group into a nearby patch of quicksand (treat as a surprise roll or fall in unless ground is prodded, effects on a 1-4/6, each player checks separately). Characters drown in 2d6 rounds unless rescued (3d6 vs. STR to escape, +1d6 each round after the first). If the characters are not drowned, the wisp heads off in search of other victims.

22. Bobblehead

A curiously-shaped white stone bobbing just beneath the surface of the water is in fact an elongated skull. The skin has withered away and a few tendons have been exposed, as has the bone. The jaw bone is particularly prominent, much more so than any other skull the characters have seen in a life of adventuring. A few wisps of hair cling to its pate. A copper coin appears to have been pushed into its empty mouth. The coin is very old and unidentifiable, while the skull has in fact been mummified by the effects produced by the swamp. Extensive digging would ultimately reveal the rest of the skeleton but would also cause a significant cave-in of the submerged branches and vegetable matter on which the adventurers walk.

23. The End is Near!

The hanging moss and drooping tree branches part to reveal a small clearing next to a moving stream of clear water. One can actually hear the sound of the water moving as it swirls past a small statue of a man in the stream channel. Fashioned from dark marble, the figure is carved with an ornate suit of armor, sword and shield. Lichen and moss cling to its base, swayed by the motion of the water rippling past. Even a few golden fish dance beneath the sunlight dappled surface as the birds sing a cheerful song above. This seems to be the only place in the swamp-land where the choking torrents of green slime and brackish water do not touch, as if it's protected by magic or another force – even the air smells fresher.

If the party follows the stream channel path, they reach the edge of the swamp and head up out of it. The trail turns gravelly and the land seems solid, no longer waterlogged. The smells are much less intense and the humidity drops noticeably. Overhead the trees thin and the sun beats down. Bird songs are fewer and more distant. Pink and purple flowers are small and hidden on the ground amid thin, pale green leaves. A few of the biting flies follow for several dozen paces, but then they too are gone. Only the mud remains, drying out in hard cakes on legs and everywhere it splattered. Of course, someone might find a leech sucking on their leg later in the day. The forest ahead is sparsely populated by very large trees and huge granite boulders, creating a maze-like atmosphere.

24. Trees and Rocks

The trail emerges from the rocks and forest into a glade. The path, which has been clear through the trees, vanishes under the vibrant plants of the meadow. Long slender leaves of various grasses cover the ground. The area where the trail leaves the meadow on the other side can be seen, leading uphill. The path up the rocky ground under the trees 100 yards away is obvious even from this distance. A straight line to the path will have the characters stepping on buttercups and iris, pushing bright flowers into the soft ground. It is squishy underfoot and water oozes into their footprints. At the center of the meadow, the area is flooded, with a few inches of water flowing over everything.

The low hill ahead has a strange shape on the top, a badly misshapen tree. The tree has gone through some terrible accident. It is split down the middle; each half now hangs out from the base of the trunk as if the tree was struck with a giant axe. Closer examination reveals obvious charring along the bark and the interior wood. The smell of burnt wood is evident, but has faded into a faint tinge in the air. The lightning that destroyed this tree did so months ago. A few feet further stands a large rock, covered with crude writing.

The large, moss-covered rock stands ten feet in height, directly ahead in the center of the path. The path goes around it on each side. Drawn in tree sap on the surface of the rock is an arrow pointing down. At the base of the rock, partially buried in the dark soil, is a roll of soft tree bark, tied with string like a scroll. Upon investigation, several crude depictions of orcs, scratched into the surface of the bark itself are obvious.

25. Goblins!

From this distance, it looks like a there is an old, ruined building of some sort sitting on top of the hill. Closer (200 feet) examination reveals that the building is a ruined temple of some sort, and from the look of things, it has been abandoned for dozens of years. Only part of one wall remains, standing grimly over the rubble strewn around the site. A single stone staircase leads six or seven feet into the air, ending at nothing. Planks and timbers stick up from the ruin randomly. The entire site is strewn with stones that vary in size from pebbles to blocks too large for anyone to lift. This ruined building is the home of 4 normal goblins, a goblin leader and a goblin shaman. There is a 50% chance during the day that they are not on guard (he fell asleep) and can be surprised on a 1-4/6. Otherwise, they have an alert guard and surprise the party on a 1-3/6.

Goblin 1—armed with a hand axe, and wears studded leather armor (1-1 HD, AC 6[13], 4 hp). He has several strips of salt pork and planks of jerked trout and a hard rye roll crusty with age and speckled with greenish mold are wrapped in a worn linen cloth (2 sp). The meager lunch is stuffed inside a dented tin drinking cup (7 cp).

Goblin 2—armed with a spear and a sling, and wears leather armor and shield (1-1 HD, AC 6[13], 5 hp). In his pocket are several coins (2 gp, 3 sp, and 8 cp), twenty sling bullets and a round, smooth white stone. The stone has chunks of other rock, dark brown and orange, imbedded in it and a hole bored through the center (2 cp).

Goblin 3—armed with a shortbow and 15 arrows, a dagger, and wears leather armor (1-1 HD, AC 7[12], 3 hp). He has a handful of coins (4 gp, 12 cp), a single-person sized loaf of bread wrapped in a cloth scrap, an S-shaped iron hook no bigger than your thumb but very strong (4 sp) and a length of white string, rolled in a ball.

Goblin 4—armed with a light crossbow, 4 quarrels and a hand axe, and wears studded leather armor and shield (1-1 HD, AC 5[14], 3 hp). He has a small leather pouch (2 gp) is embossed with a stylized bird, most likely a pheasant. The pouch is kept closed with a bone toggle, and opens to reveal four needles (5 sp each) and a small skein of milk-colored thread. A tin thimble shaped like an acorn is also in the kit (2 sp), kept in its own leather pocket.

Goblin Leader—armed with a longsword, an hand axe, and wears chainmail armor and shield (1+1 HD, AC 4[15], 8 hp). In the pocket are several coins (3 gp, 2 sp, 10 cp), a small piece of cheese wrapped in a waxed cloth and a pair of tweezers made of gray metal with enameling on the sides, showing a miniature set of flowers in a garden (6 gp). The dagger has an ornate, gilded hilt studded with blue and red gemstones and embossed in arabesque patterns. The blade itself curves back up near the point and is forged from high-quality steel. Fine writing has been engraved along the back of the blade on either side, evidently written in the language of a desert people. The blade is a +1 dagger, though its jewels (red and blue spinels) give it a slightly higher-than-normal value.

Goblin Shaman—armed with a quarterstaff, and wears studded leather armor (1 HD, AC 6[13], 4 hp). His spells are sleep, charm person and protection from good. His pockets contain handful of rough six-sided dice (5 cp), carved from cow bone within a tiny leather pouch, along with a dozen yellow and black wood tokens (1 cp total) the size of a coin and a small white ceramic container. What game they are used for, you do not know. Some of the dice are numbered normally, and others have two faces each of three colors, yellow, black and plain. Contained within the white ceramic container is a creamy white salve flecked with crushed herbs; it bears a strong, pleasant aroma of lanolin and thyme. The small jar is sealed with a silver-embossed glass screw cap. This beauty salve heals minor wounds and blemishes, instantly curing acne, boils, rashes, cuts, and similar lesions in a 2 x 2 inch area of skin for each application (which also heals 1 hit point of damage). There are a total of 12 applications remaining in the jar.

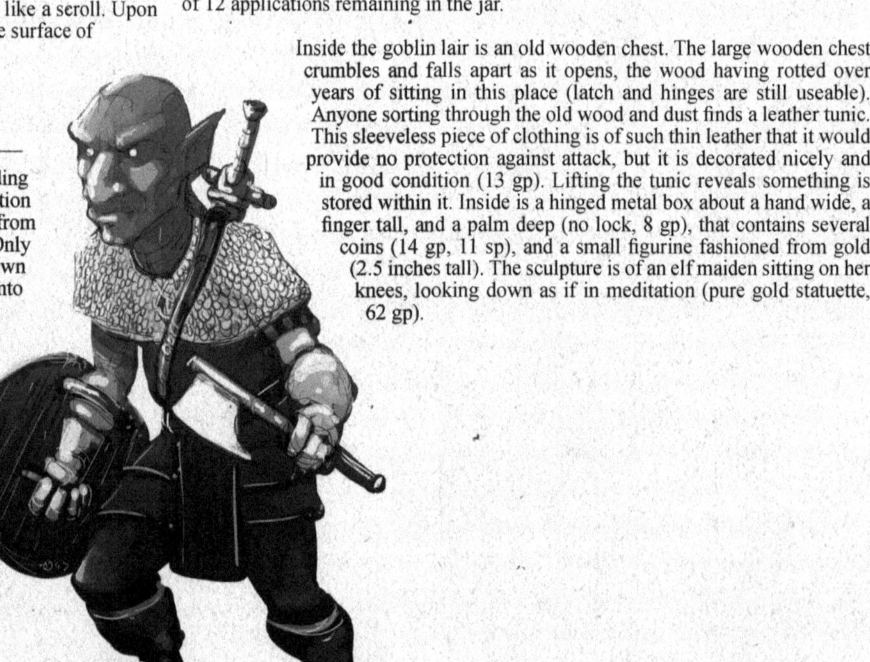

Inside the goblin lair is an old wooden chest. The large wooden chest crumbles and falls apart as it opens, the wood having rotted over years of sitting in this place (latch and hinges are still useable). Anyone sorting through the old wood and dust finds a leather tunic. This sleeveless piece of clothing is of such thin leather that it would provide no protection against attack, but it is decorated nicely and in good condition (13 gp). Lifting the tunic reveals something is stored within it. Inside is a hinged metal box about a hand wide, a finger tall, and a palm deep (no lock, 8 gp), that contains several coins (14 gp, 11 sp), and a small figurine fashioned from gold (2.5 inches tall). The sculpture is of an elf maiden sitting on her knees, looking down as if in meditation (pure gold statuette, 62 gp).

26. Another Pond

Past the ruined temple, the ground turns back to the den of rocks and huge trees, and resumes its maze-like character. Traveling along, the characters hear the sound of water, as if from a rippling stream. If the adventurers follow the sounds of the water, about fifty yards further when the sound becomes more distinct. Behind a particularly large tree is the source of the noise. About twenty yards ahead is a large pool of water, big enough to call a pond, but too small to describe as a lake. A stream is feeding the pond on the opposite side from where you stand. It seems odd that although the gurgling rivulet is running into the pool of water, there is no stream running out. Intelligent players will realize that water must be leaving the pond from somewhere, or else it would continuously rise and flood the area, which doesn't seem to be happening. There must be an egress below the surface of the water where the overflow makes its way underground to some unknown destination. (The Referee may decide that the hidden waterway pathway leads to an underground cavern or all the way to another stream that resurfaces elsewhere.) The sun holds sway here due to the size of the pond, and one can see about ten feet down into the clear water, but beyond that you can't tell how deep this pool goes. The water is fresh and drinkable. The pond is about thirty feet deep and the cavern that leads underground is at the bottom.

27. X Marks the Spot

Past the pond and down into some thick rocks is where the map indicated that the "treasure" exists. After passing through some thick undergrowth, the characters come upon a wide circular clearing. Around the edge is a ring of menhirs, each about ten feet tall and situated a few paces from the surrounding trees. The ground between the stones is an overgrown mix of clover, wildflowers and stunted berry bushes – except in the center of the clearing. The middle of the clearing is dominated by a massive slab of weathered stone, fully as wide and long as a hay wagon. The stone sits atop a mound of earth, and a circle of ground around it has been cleared down to the dirt in the recent past. The slab itself has been tipped halfway off the mound, as if someone tried to knock it from its perch, and one can see that the surface is covered in dark stains.

Hidden behind a small copse of trees 50 feet past the mound is a 4-foot diameter cave entrance leading to a small dungeon complex below. Once entered, torchlight reveals intricate stone etchings and highly detailed cave paintings depicting warfare, hunting, and even marriage rituals. No one has entered this cave for hundreds of years, as a localized landslide exposed the tunnel entrance to the outside only recently. The entrance opens into a 30-foot long, 15-foot wide cave passage, ending in a sinkhole. The sinkhole drops deep into the bowels of the earth. Warm air can be felt blowing up the hole from below. The ground inside the cave makes crunching noises when walked upon. Examination of the floor reveals that hundreds of bone fragments are mixed with the sand and gravel that make up the floor detritus.

THE DUNGEON

This small cave complex is the treasure trove indicated on the map. The dungeon itself can be expanded by the Referee if desired, and several offshoot tunnels lead to unmapped (and unwritten) areas. This allows for the Judge to add his own chambers and encounters to this area and can act as a starting point for an extended dungeon adventure if desired. As written, no wandering monsters are present here, however, if additional encounters are desired, they can certainly be added.

The cave complex contains a couple of very dangerous encounters and an ancient tomb. The traps laid by the creators of the complex are old, and often fail to function. The mechanical traps in area D (as noted in that section) are particularly affected, although the other physical hazards (and pits) still function normally.

A. THE ENTRANCE

The cavern entrance from the sinkhole above opens into a roughly 30-foot chamber with tunnels leading out to the left and right. The walls and floor are damp, and drops of water rain down sporadically from the ceiling, draining into the loose gravel floor. Bats flit about above, and guano covers the rocks and stalactites below. The floor itself is relatively even, sloping only slightly to the left. The right tunnel is dry and leads to area C, and a tiny rivulet of drainage runs down the left tunnel to area B.

B. THE WET CAVE

The tunnel opens into a large cave (60-feet in diameter) with a low ceiling (8 feet). The stone walls are stained with iron bacteria, and the cave itself is filled with 3 feet of orange colored water (from the iron). The water cascades out of the far side of the entrance, creating a splashing, waterfall like sound as it plunges down 60 feet to area F. Anyone getting within 10 feet of the waterfall area must make a save at +2 or slip and fall, and if failed, a normal save to avoid being washed over the cliff edge for 6d6 damage from the fall.

C. STONE RATS

The tunnel leads up a total of 90 feet, winding a bit to the left and ascending 40 feet in the process. The floor of the tunnel lacks much of the gravel and sand that the cave below has, and is in places smooth. Careful inspection of the floor areas reveals two small stone rat statues right at the entrance to the cave. They are perfect simulations of the small rodents, and are in fact victims of the cockatrice that lives in this cave.

The cave itself is 100 feet long and over 60 feet wide, with a tunnel exit leading to area D. The floor and ceiling have grown together with numerous stalactites and stalagmites forming columns around the room, forming a maze-like structure. Each round after the party enters the room, there is a 25% chance of encountering a large, purple and red chicken, with hellish green eyes.

Cockatrice: HD 5; AC 6[13]; Atk 1 bite (1d3 + petrification); Move 6 (Fly 18); Save 12; CL/XP 7/600; Special: Bite turns victims to stone (saving throw to avoid).

The cockatrice has no real tactics, other than pecking at intruders until they stop moving and then feeding on the soft stone created by its horrible ability. There is no treasure here. The beast fears area D, and will avoid it (having once been burned by an old trap).

D. TRICKS AND TRAPS

This cavern is 90 feet long and 30 feet wide, and appears to have been cut and carved, and is less natural than the rooms leading to it. The floor and walls are flat stone, although the ceiling itself is naturally formed. The ceiling has the usual array of stalactites, though many are broken off. Minor dust and rock detritus lies scattered across the floor.

The floor is paved with a diamond within square patterned pavers of 3 foot squares. At the 40 foot mark, there is evidence of scorching and soot staining covering a 10 foot wide swath.

Careful examination reveals a round tube is placed about knee level at this point. This is a **flame jet trap**. It is triggered by a pressure plate within the diamond patterns in line with the nozzles. If triggered, there is only a 3/6 chance that it still works. Anyone in the 10 foot section must save or take 3d6 fire damage.

Just past the flame jet trap, at the 60 foot mark, is a series of covered, counterweighted pits. Prodding these with a light pole or such will only reveal them on a 1-2/6 (the counterweights prevent easy detection). Any weight over 100 pounds placed on a pit causes it to open, requiring a save to avoid a 20 foot fall into the pit (2d6 damage). Anyone inside a pit is also trapped as the pit closes again, and must be rescued from above.

At the tunnel exit (the 90 foot mark), an additional pressure plate (this one is set in the square sections of the flooring, the diamonds are the safe route) triggers a **scything blade trap** that cuts across the 10 foot exit tunnel. This trap has a 3/6 chance to function, and requires a save to avoid taking 6d6 damage to anyone within its path. Careful examination of the wall inside the tunnel reveals the blades (set between two sets of stones on either side of the tunnel).

E. THE TOMB

This small room has been completely finished with stonework. The room itself is 30 feet square, with a 12 foot ceiling. The walls are painted with intricate scenes and hieroglyphs of some ancient make. A *read languages* spell or a thief using his read languages ability can discern that this is the tomb of a high priest of the god Set. The writing on the wall contains various unsavory scenes related to Set's dismembering of Osiris and of foul rites performed in his service. The writing contains a series of prayers to the dark god and promises to serve him in the underworld by the deceased.

In the center of this chamber is a 12 foot long, 5 foot wide stone sarcophagus in the Egyptian style. It is quite heavy to open (requires pry bars and at least 3 characters). Inside is an (inanimate) mummy. The mummy wears a death mask of pure silver (worth 1500 gp), and a golden broach inset with various semiprecious stones (250 gp). Near the mummy's feet are 6 canopic jars carved of various materials and decorated (worth 100 gp each), and a *Manual of Wisdom*. If the characters dump oil and blaze immediately (thinking mummy), the book is lost.

While the mummy is inert, there is a curse on anyone disturbing the mummy's rest. Three rounds after any portion of the mummy or the canopic jars are removed from the sarcophagus, a Category I Demon is summoned to the chamber. The demon fights for only 6 rounds (effectively a monster summoning V spell), then disappears.

Vrock: HD 8; AC 1[18]; Atk 1 beak (1d6) and 2 foreclaws (1d4) and rear claws (1d6); Move 12 (Fly 18); Save 8; CL/XP 9/1100; Special: Create darkness (5' radius), immune to fire, magic resistance (50%).

F. The Waterfall Chamber

This large cave is very wet, and consists of many pools and ledges dropping to lower pools. The cavern itself is over 300 feet in diameter, and water flows in from above (from area B as well as wilderness area 26). An underground river flows through the far edge of the cavern. It is swiftly flowing and deep. No monsters or other dangers (other than possibly drowning or falling) are present.

The Referee can either end the adventure here or add his own material to the cave. Perhaps there are multiple exits from the cave? Maybe the river leads deeper into the earth to areas that can be explored? Either way, this ends this module, and we hope you have enjoyed it!

ADVENTURES
WORTH
WINNING